MW01275355

Creepy Crawlies

Bloodsucking Lice and Fleas

Ellen Rodger

Crabtree Publishing Company

www.crabtreebooks.com

**Developed and produced by
Plan B Book Packagers**

Author & Editorial director:
Ellen Rodger

Art director:
Rosie Gowsell-Pattison

Logo design:
Margaret Amy Salter

Editor:
Molly Aloian

Proofreader:
Crystal Sikkens

Project manager:
Kathy Middleton

**Production coordinator
& prepress technician**:
Katherine Berti

Photographs:
ChrisTrip Photos: Chris Tripodi: p. 20
Rose Gowsell-Pattison/Plan B Book Packagers: p. 16–17
Robert Hooke (1635-1703) Diagram of a louse: p. 9 (bottom)
Istockphoto: cover, p. 15; Arlindo71: p. 14; Kevin Dyer:
    p. 10 (bottom left), 21 (top), 25 (top); spxChrome: p. 3
Nzfooty: p. 7 (top)
Photos.com: cover, logo
Roebot: p. 26
Shutterstock: cover, p. 1–2, 9 (top); 3drenderings: p. 13 (middle);
    Nuno Andre: p. 25 (inset); Andrjuss: p. 4 (bottom left);
    Blamb: p. 6 (top); Jorge Pedro Barradas de Casais: p. 24;
    Dolnikov Denys: p. 10 (bottom right); Dragon Fang:
     p. 28 (bottom); Bonnie Fink: p. 6 (bottom); Forest Path:
    p. 27 (top); Galinka: p. 19; Brendan Howard: p. 12; Petar
    Ivanov Ishmiriev: p. 25 (bottom); Sergey Kamshylin:
    p. 5 (top); Matin: p. 4 (bottom right); Miramiska:
    p. 13 (top and bottom); Monkey Business Images:
    p. 21 (bottom); Motorolka: p. 23 (right); Andreas Nilsson:
    p. 29 (bottom); Martine Oger: p. 8; Pandapaw: p. 11;
    Paul Matthew Photography: p. 28 (top); Nikolai Pozdeev:
    p. 23 (top); Ljupco Smokovski: p. 27 (bottom); Christie
    Spear: p. 18; Surabhi25: p. 22 (middle); Tlorna: p. 4 (top);
    Tomasz Trojanowski: p. 22 (bottom); Chad Zuber:
    p. 5 (bottom)

Library and Archives Canada Cataloguing in Publication

Rodger, Ellen
    Bloodsucking lice and fleas / Ellen Rodger.

(Creepy crawlies)
Includes index.
ISBN 978-0-7787-2498-8 (bound).--ISBN 978-0-7787-2505-3 (pbk.)

    1. Lice--Juvenile literature. 2. Fleas--Juvenile literature.
3. Lice as carriers of disease--Juvenile literature. 4. Fleas as
carriers of disease--Juvenile literature. I. Title.
II. Series: Creepy crawlies (St. Catharines, Ont).

QL540.R62 2010   j595.7'56   C2010-901754-4

Library of Congress Cataloging-in-Publication Data

Rodger, Ellen.
 Bloodsucking lice and fleas / Ellen Rodger.
    p. cm. -- (Creepy crawlies)
 Includes index.
 ISBN 978-0-7787-2498-8 (reinforced lib. bdg. : alk. paper)
-- ISBN 978-0-7787-2505-3 (pbk. : alk. paper)
 1. Lice as carriers of disease--Juvenile literature. 2. Fleas as carriers of disease-
-Juvenile literature. 3. Lice--Juvenile literature. 4. Fleas--Juvenile literature. I.
Title. II. Series.

 RA641.L6R63 2011
 614.4'324--dc22
                                        2010009549

Crabtree Publishing Company

www.crabtreebooks.com   1-800-387-7650

Printed in China/072010/AP20100226

**Published in Canada
Crabtree Publishing**
616 Welland Ave.
St. Catharines, Ontario
L2M 5V6

**Published in the United States
Crabtree Publishing**
PMB 59051
350 Fifth Avenue, 59th Floor
New York, New York 10118

**Published in the United Kingdom
Crabtree Publishing**
Maritime House
Basin Road North, Hove
BN41 1WR

**Published in Australia
Crabtree Publishing**
386 Mt. Alexander Rd.
Ascot Vale (Melbourne)
VIC 3032

Contents

The Cooties!

They feed on us, make their homes on us, and make our lives miserable. They are horrible guests, sometimes spreading deadly diseases. These bloodsucking **ectoparasites** are lice and fleas and they are pests of the first order!

Small But Mighty

Lice are wingless insects that live on the bodies of humans. They feed on human blood and lay their eggs in hair. Fleas are pesky insect vampires that live on and make meals of animals. They attach themselves to animal hair and use their spectacular jumping skills to find new prey. Some flea species are even partial to humans! Lice and fleas are tiny. Adult lice are about the size of a sesame seed! Fleas are no more than 1/8 of an inch (3.3 mm) long. Both lice and fleas are **adapted** to living on human or animal **hosts**. They affect millions of people and animals around the globe each year.

Lice can make your entire head and body itch, yet they are only about the size of a sesame seed on a hamburger bun.

CRAWLY FACT

Getting the "Cooties"

Almost everyone has heard of the term "cooties." In schoolyards, the cooties is usually thought of as an imaginary disease spread by mere contact with a person. The cooties are in fact, real. During **World War I**, soldiers in Europe fought and lived close together in mud trenches. Cooties was a slang term they used to describe the head and body lice **infestations** that broke out and contributed to their misery. Sometimes, soldiers would be so infested that they were crawling with lice. There was very little they could do except try to flick them off or crush the lice with their fingernails.

Itchy and Scratchy

Lice and fleas are annoying for their hosts. Their bloodsucking leaves victims itchy. No amount of scratching can relieve the constant itch and the endless scratching can lead to skin infections. Some people and animals also have **allergic reactions** to lice and flea saliva and waste. These can be nasty, causing flu-like symptoms. Anyone can get lice. They are not picky. They live on clean heads and bodies just as easily as on dirty ones. All that is required is close contact between people. Fleas are equally nasty to their hosts. Ever wonder why your pet scratches itself raw? It might be fleas! Fleabites appear as lines or clusters and can stay itchy for weeks. Fleas can also spread deadly diseases to humans such as the **bubonic plague** and **typhus**.

Just thinking about lice and fleas can give you the creeps and force you to scratch your head or body. Why do these tiny flightless insects make people so fearful and frustrated?

Moochers and Latchers

Lice cannot live long without a human or animal host. Fleas can go longer without a meal, but they prefer to be well fed. The primary goal of lice is to find food—and that means us! Human lice suck blood and inject saliva into the skin. This causes the human body to respond, making the site itchy. These uninvited guests can also be difficult to get rid of. Lice have six legs and strong claws for latching onto hosts.

A single female louse can lay about 100 eggs. Its easy to see how a person can be crawling with lice! Female fleas can lay more than 500 eggs in their two week lifetime.

Lice and fleas have been around for millions of years and are not likely to disappear. In fact, cases of human head lice are on the rise, and some health professionals believe this is due to lice adapting to the chemical treatments developed over the last 50 years to get rid of the pests.

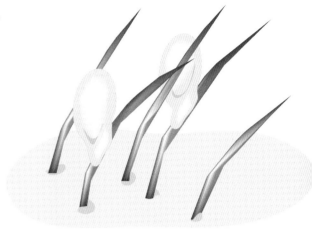

A host's hair makes a perfect spot to lay eggs. Female lice stick the eggs to hair shafts.

Lice and fleas can be "picky." Some species are adapted to specific hosts. Despite living in a harsh Arctic environment, even polar bears get fleas.

Feeling Lousy?

Human head lice are not known to cause diseases, but body lice are a vector, or an organism that transfers disease from one living thing to another. During World War I, body lice transferred trench fever, also known as five day fever, from soldier to soldier. The fever did not kill, but was like a miserable cold or flu. Body lice are also known to transmit bacteria that cause other diseases. Fleas are known to have transmitted plagues that caused millions of deaths.

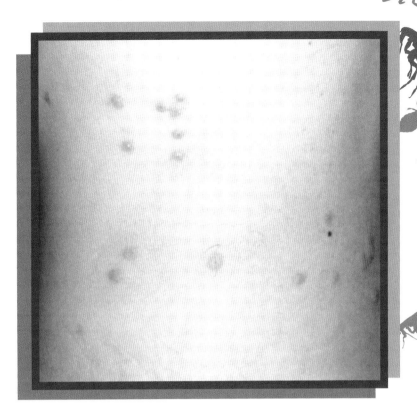

Cat fleas, the most common type in most households, will feed on other hosts, including humans. The bites appear as red bumps on the skin.

THAT'S CREEPY

Itching All Over

Only three types of lice feed and breed on humans: body lice, head lice, and **pubic** lice. Body lice and head lice look almost the same, but their habitat, or their natural environment, is different. Body lice live on the body, attached to hair in places such as the armpits, chest, or legs. They can also hide in the seams of clothing. Head lice live on the head and neck, and often get into clothing such as hats and scarves. Pubic lice resemble tiny crabs because of their rounder bodies and larger front legs. They live in the pubic area.

A Lousy History

For much of human history, lice and fleas were commonplace. As ectoparasites, fleas and lice have lived with, **evolved**, and adapted to their hosts over millions of years. Lice eggs, called nits, have even been found in **archeological** digs of **prehistoric** burial sites. Like their wild relatives, **domestic** animals routinely suffered from fleas. Until recently, there was no such thing as flea shots and collars, or delousing powders and shampoos. Humans accepted that lice and fleas were an ordinary part of living but they did what they could to relieve their suffering.

Cats were much-loved and occasionally worshiped in Ancient Egypt. The cat flea was a constant presence. Even "hairless" cats such as the Sphynx, which has fine hair, get fleas.

Ancient Pests

The Ancient Egyptians were known to have battled lice by shaving their heads and wearing wigs. Wigs could, of course, still be crawling with lice, but removed from a source of food (a head to bite), lice died. They could also be spotted on a bald head. To be "clean" for religious rituals, Egyptian priests were known to have shaved their entire bodies, including their eyebrows! This made priests the least likely people to have lice. Folk remedies for fleas and lice were also well known. The *Eber Papyrus*, an ancient Egyptian medical text, recommended chewing date meal with water and spitting it on the skin as a cure for lice and flea infestations. No one knows if this actually worked. Ancient Egyptians also used natron, a mineral salt found in dried lake beds, to repel fleas.

Whacky Reasoning

The history of lice and fleas is a history of strange cures, wacky reasoning on why lice and fleas occur, and preventative potions. People did not understand that lice and fleas were parasitic insects. They afflicted people more when they lived in crowded conditions, as most people did. Many ancient peoples believed lice were spontaneously created from human sweat. Greek writer and philosopher Aristotle (384 BC–322 BC) wrote that lice developed from the "flesh of animals." Aristotle also believed that some people were more prone to having body lice because they sweated more, and that women had more lice than men. Aristotle's idea that lice emerged from flesh is called spontaneous generation. It was an idea that many people believed until scientist **Louis Pasteur** proved it was wrong in 1864.

Wigs were worn by wealthy men and women in the 1600s and 1700s. Often, the hair underneath had lice.

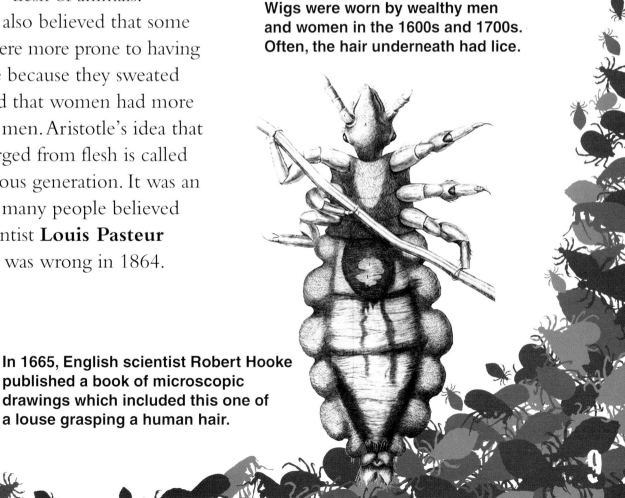

In 1665, English scientist Robert Hooke published a book of microscopic drawings which included this one of a louse grasping a human hair.

Early Remedies

In his travels through Asia, explorer Marco Polo wrote about how wealthy Indians slept in beds raised from the floor as a way of escaping fleas. The ancient Chinese developed effective flea and lice killing powders, lotions, and potions. One such remedy used arsenic, a chemical that is poisonous to humans and other animals. They also developed plant-based **insecticides** and **parasiticides**. One of the most common historical remedies for lice is the comb. By combing through hair, people could look for and remove nits. They could also crush live adult lice. Combing for nits is still used as one remedy for lice.

Lice and fleas became easier to see when the magnifying glass was invented in 1250.

Nit combs have long teeth for pulling lice off hair. Many insecticides kill lice but are harmful to human health.

Before dying, people infected with the bubonic plague developed swollen glands called buboes, and red or black spots on their skin. At the time, nobody knew that the disease was caused by bacteria spread by rat fleas.

The Plague

The reputation of fleas was permanently sealed when, in 1894, scientists discovered that they were responsible for the spread of the deadliest disease in history. The bubonic plague, or the Black Death, swept through Europe in 1347, leaving millions dead. The plague was spread through Europe by rats infected with a bacteria called Yersinia pestis. The rats were infected with the bacteria through their fleas. Infected fleas transmitted the Yersinia pestis bacteria by regurgitating infected blood into their rat hosts. When their rat hosts died, the fleas started biting people for food, transmitting the bacteria to them.

THAT'S CREEPY

Even the first president of the United States could not escape lice.

Crawling With Them

Until about the early 1900s, almost everybody was bothered by lice and fleas at some time in their lives. In the 1700s, when people bathed less often and there were no chemical insecticides, lice and fleas were an acknowledged and accepted part of life. Head scratching was often a sign of infestation. Many people considered it improper to scratch your head while at the dinner table or in public. While still a teenager, George Washington wrote a book on manners. In his *Rules for Civility and Decent Behaviour in Company and Conversation*, Washington advises not to kill fleas and lice in front of people, as it was considered rude.

There are over 3,000 species of lice and over 2,300 species of fleas. Each species has specific characteristics. Some are biters and some are suckers. Some only attach themselves to a specific animal. All are ectoparasites, which means they live externally, or on the outside of their host's body. Elephants get lice, fish get lice, and even plants get lice. Elephant lice (*Haematomyzus elephantis*) are host specific. They live only on the hair and skin of elephants. The human flea (*Pulex irritans*) is not so fussy. It feeds off a wide host **spectrum**, from humans to monkeys, and pigs.

Classification

It is not always easy to identify a species of louse or flea just by examining it with the naked eye. Biologists group and categorize organisms such as lice and fleas using a system called taxonomy. The system was originally set up by Swedish biologist Carl Linnaeus in 1738. It has been altered and corrected for scientific accuracy since that time.

Many biologists have since improved upon the taxonomy introduced by Carl Linnaeus.

A Kingdom Of... Fleas?

Linnaeus grouped animals and plants into broad kingdoms and then divided them into ranks that made living things easy to identify. Today, the system has been corrected to classify living things according to a system of common descent. Kingdoms are divided into groups called phyla, based on body structure, class, family, genus, and species.

Better Known As...

Linnaeus is best known for his method of naming species using shortened Latin names. Cat fleas, or *Ctenocephalides felis,* are a separate species from dog fleas (*Ctenocephalides canis*) and the oriental rat flea (*Xenopsylla cheopis*). Entomologists are still studying the relationships between the species. Lice belong to the Phthiraptera order. There are at least four suborders, including Anoplura, which are sucking lice consisting of head, body, and pubic lice, Rhyncophthirina, the parasitic lice of elephants and warthogs, Ischnocera, or avian lice, that are specific to birds, and Amblycera, or chewing lice.

Fleas belong to the Animalia kingdom, the Arthropoda phylum, Insecta class, and Pulicidae family. Fleas are insects of the Siphonaptera order, meaning they are wingless and have mouthparts for piercing and sucking.

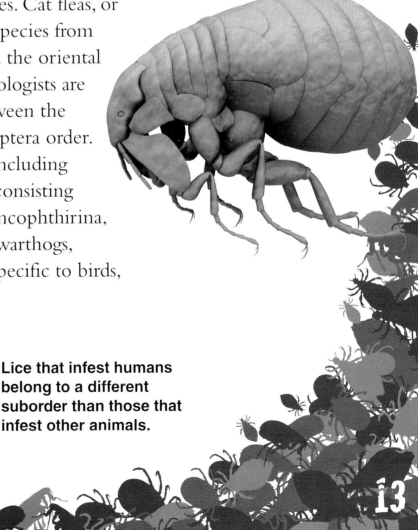

Lice that infest humans belong to a different suborder than those that infest other animals.

Anatomy Lesson

Lice and fleas are wingless and therefore cannot fly, but they manage to travel very efficiently from host to host. Head lice travel from person to person through head to head contact or through clothing such as hats. Lice crawl onto hosts and then latch onto hair. Fleas are fantastic jumpers. They use their powerful hind legs to leap up to 7 inches (17.8 cm) in the air or 13 inches (33 cm) horizontally. This makes traveling from host to host, or ground to host, a cinch.

Lice have antennae and eyes for sensing a host's scalp.

Lice have six legs which end in claws. These legs are attached to the thorax between the head and abdomen.

Head lice appear yellow to grey on a host's head. They have hard, flat bodies.

Lice have mouthparts that can pierce skin and suck blood. When not in use, the mouthparts are retracted into the louse's head.

Lice breathe through spiracles, or small openings, on the abdomen.

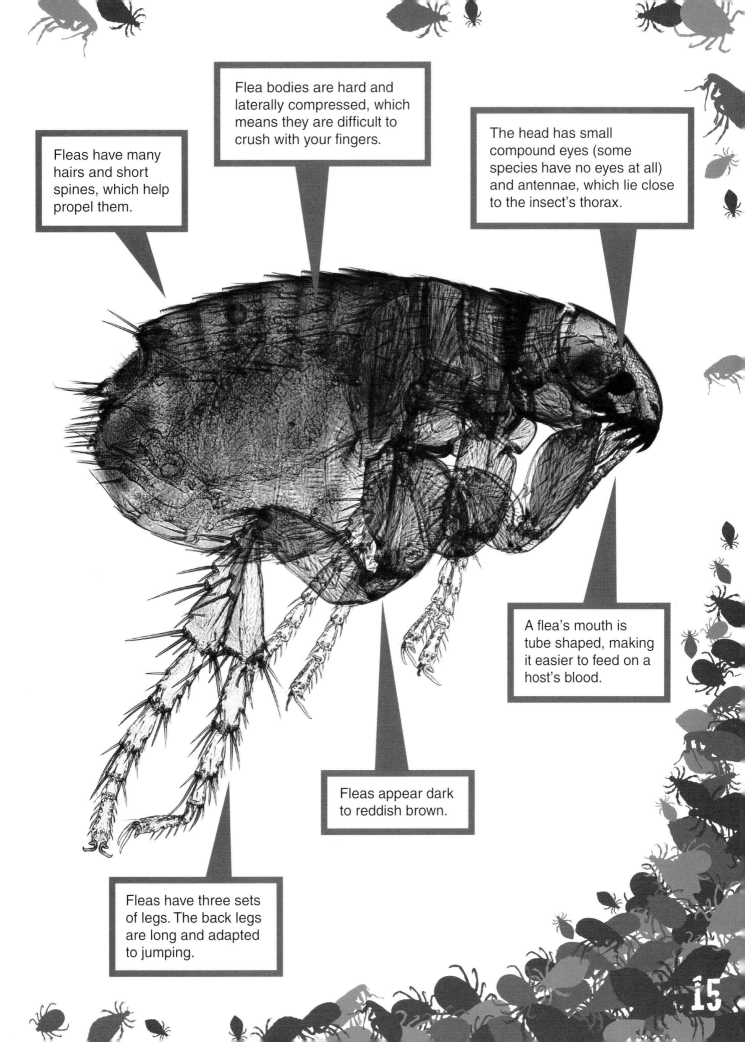

Fleas have many hairs and short spines, which help propel them.

Flea bodies are hard and laterally compressed, which means they are difficult to crush with your fingers.

The head has small compound eyes (some species have no eyes at all) and antennae, which lie close to the insect's thorax.

A flea's mouth is tube shaped, making it easier to feed on a host's blood.

Fleas appear dark to reddish brown.

Fleas have three sets of legs. The back legs are long and adapted to jumping.

Life Cycles

Unfortunately for fluffy, fleas are remarkably long-lived critters. Some species take 30 days to complete their life cycles. Others take many months to complete their life cycles. They hatch from eggs and develop into larvae, then pupae, and then adults. Flea eggs are laid on a host. Adult female fleas can lay up to 50 eggs a day.

Flea eggs are not secured to the animal's hair, like lice nits are. They often fall off the animal onto carpets and furniture. They may even be in the blanket the dog rests on.

From Larva With Love

The larval stage for a flea lasts five to eighteen days. Larvae go through three development stages before they spin cocoons and become pupae. Pupae can emerge in three to five days, or they can remain in the cocoon for over a year, depending on outside circumstances, such as humidity. They emerge from the cocoon as adults.

Lice Cycle

Head lice take about one month to complete their life cycles. Nymphs hatch from nits, and develop into adults. Nits are laid by female lice in the base of a host's hair shaft. The host's head provides the warmth needed to **incubate** the nits. The nymphs grow and **molt** out of their **exoskeletons** three times before they become adults. This process takes about seven to ten days.

From Nit to Louse

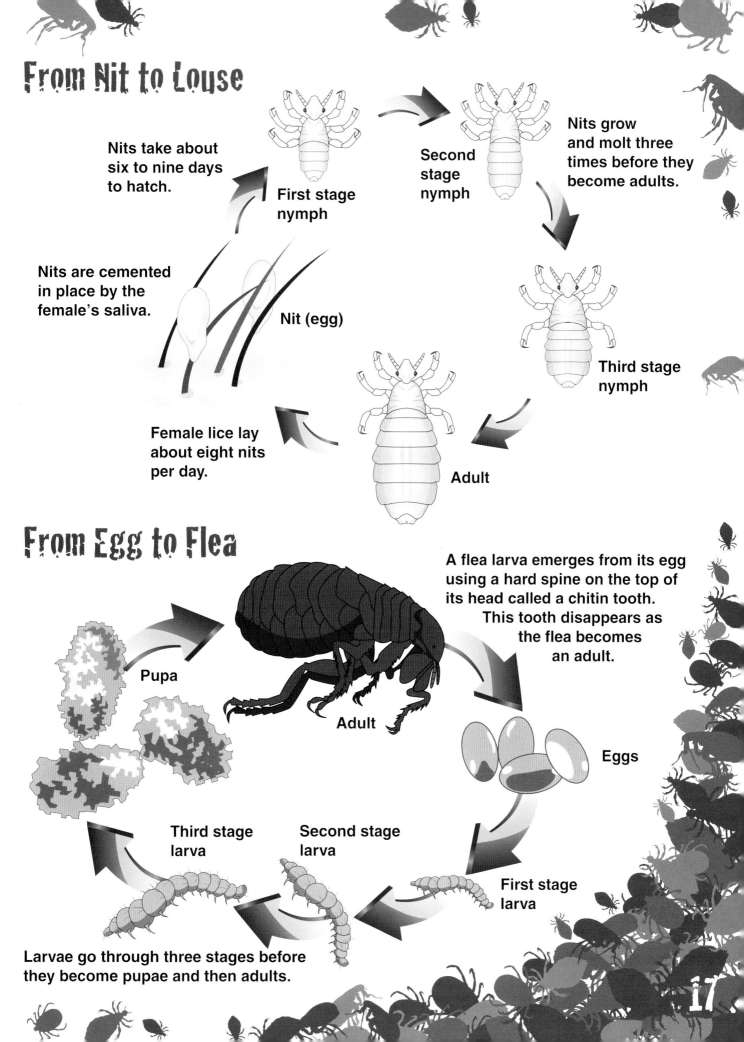

Nits take about six to nine days to hatch.

First stage nymph

Second stage nymph

Nits grow and molt three times before they become adults.

Nits are cemented in place by the female's saliva.

Nit (egg)

Third stage nymph

Female lice lay about eight nits per day.

Adult

From Egg to Flea

Pupa

Adult

A flea larva emerges from its egg using a hard spine on the top of its head called a chitin tooth. This tooth disappears as the flea becomes an adult.

Eggs

Third stage larva

Second stage larva

First stage larva

Larvae go through three stages before they become pupae and then adults.

17

Flea Bags

The world is an enormous place for a flea. Luckily, there are plenty of hosts to grab a meal from and make a home on.

Lying Low

Fleas are survivors. From the time larvae emerge from their eggs, they are on their own. Larvae are blind and legless, and must avoid harsh light. They feed on the bits of skin and other food they find in their surroundings. This includes flea **feces**, which is composed of blood, bits of vegetable matter, and dead insects. Well-fed larvae pupate after their larval stages. Pupal fleas can spend weeks or even months in their protective cocoons. They emerge when they sense the carbon dioxide expelled in the breath of a nearby host.

Fleas live in animal environments.

Walking Flea Motel

Many pet owners believe their animals are "clean" and will not get fleas. They are wrong! A flea's natural habitat is a dog or cat's fur. Even the cleanest indoor dog or cat is **susceptible** to fleas if they are unprotected. After they emerge from the cocoon, fleas only have about a week to find food. They are focused and skilled at finding a host. When a host appears, they latch onto the host's hair. They crawl down to the host's skin to feed and lay their eggs. Fleas then stick with the host or live close to where the host sleeps or lays.

A Flea For All

There are about 2,000 species of fleas. Some are adapted to single hosts and will not feed on any others. Other fleas are opportunists. They may prefer a meal of cat blood, but will suck on dogs and humans, as well. The fleas that live on domestic animals like it warm and moist. Eggs need humidity to hatch and larvae need a warm, moist environment to grow.

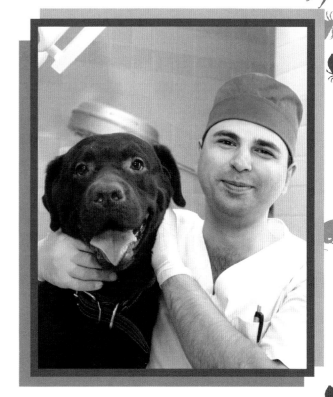

Flea season is usually early spring to late fall. Fleas like warm, moist weather. Veterinarians like to keep animals free of fleas.

CRAWLY FACT

Fevers, Sickness, and Death

Most people think of the plague as a disease that killed people in the Middle Ages, when there was little knowledge of what caused it and how to treat it. But the plague still exists and fleas still transfer it to animals and humans. According to the World Health Organization, between 1,000 and 3,000 cases of the plague are reported each year. The fleas of flying squirrels also transfer a bacteria that causes murine typhus. Murine typhus is a disease that causes a rash, fever, severe pain, and often death, if untreated.

Nitpicking

In the days before chemical treatments for lice, people combed through the heads of those who had lice. Nits were located one by one and picked from the scalp. This process, called nitpicking, is still practiced today. Nitpicking is detailed work that requires a keen eye, a steady hand, and nerves of steel.

More than One Meaning

Today, when a person is called a nitpicker, it often means they are fussy and overly critical. Nitpickers use their hands and combs to examine a head and find lice and nits. The expression "going through things with a fine tooth comb" refers to the comb used by nitpickers to separate hairs near the scalp. These combs were difficult to brush through to the ends of thick hair but good for helping to dislodge nits that were cemented to hair roots.

Nitpicking used to be a normal part of grooming for humans. Some animals also groom for lice and fleas.

This nit comb has long, narrow teeth and a mirrored handle for seeing lice and nits.

Signs of Lice

A lice infestation is called pediculosis. There are tell-tale signs of head lice. Often a host's head will be itchy from lice bites and from the movement of the **parasites**. Nits might be visible around the ears or nape of the neck. Head lice are not a sign of poor hygiene. It does not mean the person who has lice is dirty. Lice are adapted to human heads. It is their natural environment. For thousands of years, they were a normal part of life. Nitpicking and combing were some of the first and most natural ways to combat lice. Today, nitpickers sometimes wear disposable gloves and examine heads in good light. Hair should be examined in sections and combed. Fine tooth, or nit combs with long thin teeth, are designed to remove lice, nymphs, and nits. Once removed, the nits can be washed away in a sink, and the comb disinfected.

One sure way to eliminate head lice is to shave your head. Lice have adapted claws to hang on to hair, but their claws are useless against a bald head.

Potions and Poisons

For thousands of years, people have battled lice and fleas with diligence and a number of weapons, including natural potions. Lice treatments included ointments made from cedar sap, lard, herbs, and minerals. Flea treatments included using peppermint oil and eating garlic. Many ancient treatments were creepier than lice and fleas. Roman philosopher Pliny the Elder advised eating snake skins and using stavesacre seeds to get rid of lice. Stavesacre is an herb, also called lice bane. Bane is an old-fashioned word for poison. Stavesacre seeds are used in ointments. Unfortunately, the herb can be toxic to more than just lice.

Some people believe mayonnaise and olive oil kill lice, but there is no proof.

Folk Remedies

There are plenty of folk remedies for lice and fleas. The Center for Disease Control (CDC) cautions that there is no evidence that folk remedies work. In tests done by the center, treatments using mayonnaise, vinegar, olive oil, alcohol, butter, and petroleum jelly were proven ineffective against head lice. Lice were able to survive prolonged soaking in water for up to eight hours.

Lice infested clothing needs to be washed in hot water.

Flea baths are a common method for controlling fleas on pets. Pets can also wear flea collars, or get preventative pills from a veterinarian.

Stronger Solutions

Pyrethrum is a mixture made with chrysanthemum flower seeds. In the 1940s, people began using pyrethrum as an insecticide and delousing powder. Pyrethrins are still used today but with caution, as they can be toxic. Synthetic pesticides came into widespread use in the mid–1940s. They were effective at killing lice and fleas, but some of them had horrible effects on the environment as they also killed other animals.

Chemical Treatments

Today, there are many chemical treatments for lice and fleas such as shampoos. These shampoos are extremely harsh on the skin and immune systems of children. Anything strong enough to kill a pest can be harmful to humans if used incorrectly, or too often. Lice are great adapters. They have also developed **resistence** to many insecticides. This has led to a resurgence in infestations.

Predators and Prey

The fleas and lice that prey on humans and domestic animals have no natural predators, except their frustrated hosts. Lice grooming is common behavior for animals. Birds use their beaks to peck away at pesky lice and fleas. Apes and monkeys groom each other, and eat any errant lice they happen upon. Dogs and cats bite and scratch away fleas and crush them with their teeth.

Why Me?

Lice are a fact of life. Many humans who have not been the victims of a lice infestation wonder why they seem to attack children more often than adults. The answer lies in the behavior of children. Pediculosis is endemic, which means it is a condition that always exists somewhere in the population. Most kids who get lice, get them at school where they are more likely to have their heads close together. Some heads are more difficult to **colonize**. African American hair is more oval shaped and the lice species that is most common in North America has trouble latching on. This makes it harder for the lice, but not impossible.

Lice affect children aged three to twelve far more often than adults. Children have a higher risk because they often work or play with their heads close together.

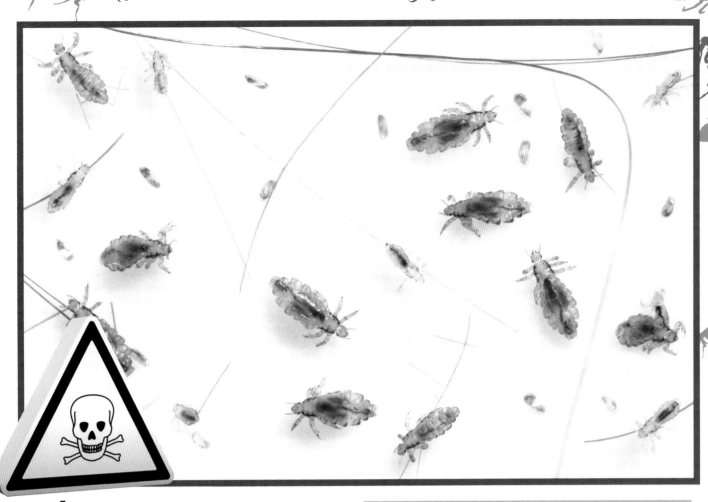

We're Baaack!

Widespread use of chemical pesticides meant that lice and flea outbreaks were less common from 1945 to 1978. The synthetic pesticide DDT was banned in the United States in 1973 because it was linked to the deaths of other animals in the food chain and to certain cancers. In their ongoing struggle to survive, lice have also developed resistence to other treatments.

(top) Lice cling to narrow hair strands. They are survivors that always adapt.

(right) A bird pecks at lice.

Flea Fascination

Ectoparasites use humans and animals for food, places to live, and places to lay their eggs. It's no wonder these tiny creatures take up such a large space in our imagination. They are the subject of many stories, books, poems, and events.

FLEA CIRCUS

Flea circuses were once major circus sideshow attractions. Fleas were tied to decorated carts and small platforms where they did "tricks." People watched the circus behind a special magnifying lense. Fleas were attached to props that made them appear to be trained at tricks such as juggling or playing instruments. Flea circuses lost their appeal around the 1950s and today there are very few flea circuses.

Fleas circus "performers" often only live a few months.

FEELING LOUSY?

The term "feeling lousy," used by people to say they are feeling low or in ill health, began as a description of the itchiness of pediculosis, or head-lice infestation. Louse is also a term used to describe a rotten person. Calling something lousy is a way of saying it was bad.

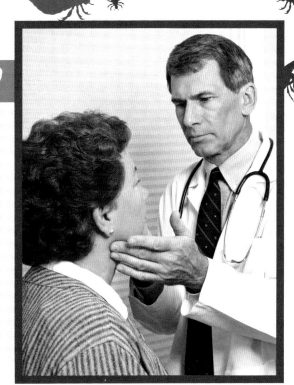

FLEA MARKET

Flea markets are a type of bazaar where second-hand items are sold. The name "flea market" is thought to have come from the fact that some of the merchandise sold at the markets was infested with fleas.

TO A LOUSE

The poem, "To A Louse," written by Scottish poet Robert Burns in 1785, describes how a louse is spied on the bonnet of a well-dressed woman at church. The louse is called an "ugly, creeping, blasted wonner (wonder)" that is "detested by saint and sinner."

Lousy Critters

Lice and fleas are pretty creepy, but they are also interesting organisms. Both are highly specialized insects that prey on specific hosts. They are a subject of study for entomologists who examine parasites, and health care experts who follow their impact on human and animal populations. Want to know more about lice and fleas? Read on:

The word ukelele means "jumping flea" in the Hawaiian language. The name comes from how the fingers of skilled ukelele players appear to jump on the strings.

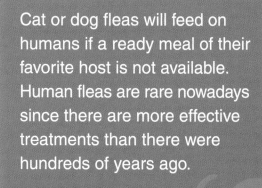

Cat or dog fleas will feed on humans if a ready meal of their favorite host is not available. Human fleas are rare nowadays since there are more effective treatments than there were hundreds of years ago.

Delusional parasitosis, or Ekbom's Syndrome, is a disorder that causes a person to believe that he or she is infested with parasites such as lice. People with delusional parasitosis have **hallucinations** in which their skin is crawling. The disorder often happens to people addicted to certain drugs.

Fleas have been around for about 100 million years. They have been found in fossil remains from the Cretaceous period—the time of the dinosaurs.

Flea feces is called "flea dirt" and it is mostly made up of dried blood. Looking for flea dirt on your dog or cat is one way to confirm a flea infestation. Flea dirt looks like tiny black spots visible on your pet's hair when it is parted.

Body lice is most common when humans live in crowded conditions, are unable to change their clothing regularly, and huddle together, such as after disasters and wars.

Pest Detective

Nobody will recommend that you get up close and personal with lice and fleas, but there are plenty of other ways to study the ectoparasites. Check out the following resources to find out more about how they live and adapt, and how to prevent an infestation of lice and fleas.

WEB SITES

Here are some cool sites to check out:

The National Pediculosis Association
www.headlice.org
This is a site dedicated to teaching about head lice and giving readers the most up-to-date information on lice research and treatment. Read about lice removal products, and find information on lice anatomy and habitats. A special kids section has games, poetry, and animated images.

Center for Disease Control
www.cdc.gov/lice/
This Web site provides information on lice and fleas and their risks to human health. Topics include descriptions of risk factors, diagnosis, treatment, and cures. This is a good facts-based site for school reports and papers.

Pestworld
www.pestworldforkids.org
This is a site set up by the National Pest Management Association to promote professional pest control. It provides information on pests such as lice and fleas and gives suggestions on how to write reports and do science fair projects. A pest guide gives clear information on size, habitat, and diet, as well as listing the kingdom, species, family, and class the insect belongs to.

Here are some great books on lice, fleas, and other insects:

Head Lice, by Jason Glaser.
Capstone Press, 2006.

Lice: Head Hunters, by Barbara A. Somervill.
Powerkids Press, 2007.

Flea, by Karen Hartly, Chris Macro, and Philip Taylor.
Heinemann Library, 2008.

The ABCs of Insects, by Bobbie Kalman.
Crabtree Publishing Company, 2009.

The World of Insects series.
Crabtree Publishing Company, 2005

Want to see lice and fleas up close and personal? Here are some great places to visit:

American Museum of Natural History
Central Park West at 79th Street
New York, NY 10024-5192
Phone: (212) 769-5100

The Montreal Insectarium
4581 Sherbrooke East
Montréal, Québec, Canada, H1X 2B2
Phone: (514) 872-1400

Invertebrate Exhibit, The National Zoo
3001 Connecticut Ave., NW
Washington, DC 20008
Phone: (540) 635-6500

The O. Orkin Insect Zoo at the National Museum of Natural History, Smithsonian
10th Street and Constitution Ave., NW
Washington, DC 20560
Phone: (202) 633-1000

Glossary

adapted Adjusted to new conditions

allergic reactions Responses by the body's immune system to a foreign substance. This can mean anything from rashes to difficulty breathing and severe illness

archeological Something related to early or prehistoric history

bubonic plague A severe illness that causes fever, buboes, or swollen glands in the neck or groin, and often death

colonize To establish in an area

domestic A tame animal or one kept by humans

ectoparasite An organism that lives on and feeds off of the outside of a host

evolved Developed and changed to suit the environment over many generations

exoskeleton A hard external covering that provides support and protection for invertebrates

feces Waste matter

hallucinations Feelings or things of which one is aware, but which are not real; usually the result of a mental disorder, or the effect of a drug

host An animal on which a parasite lives

incubate To develop in a warm environment

infestation To be overrun with insects

insecticides Substances used for killing insects

Louis Pasteur A French microbiologist (1822-1895) who is known for his work on disease causes and prevention

molt Shedding a body or skin to make way for new growth

parasites Living things that live on or in other living things

parasiticides A substance used in medicine to kill parasites

prehistoric Before the time of written records

pubic Relating to the area near the genitals

resistence Immune or not vulnerable to something

spectrum A range

susceptible Likely to be attacked or harmed

typhus An infectious disease caused by bacteria spread by fleas and some lice species

World War I A major war fought in Europe from 1914 to 1918 where the Central Powers (Germany, Austria-Hungary) were defeated by Britain and its allies Canada, Australia, New Zealand, and later Italy and the United States

Index